SISSIES GENDER-SWAPPED ON HALLOWEEN

First Time Sissification Anthology

Leandra Camilli

CONTENTS

GENDER SWAPPING MY HUSBAND'S GAY LOVER

A First Time Sissification Halloween Story

CHAPTER 1

Nothing quite like fucking a married man, I thought, loving how his balls were slapping off my butt. He was behind me, his fingers digging into my skin. Claude was a beast of a man and was controlling everything I was doing, including my breathing.

Laughs, chatters, and music echoed into the room as they reminded me we weren't alone. Anyone could walk up to the door, hear the sounds we were making, and wonder what was happening. If they weren't retards, they'd figure it out before long.

I wasn't worried about that, focusing on the hard, massive cock pounding in and out of me. Nothing quite like it, his muscles bulging and straining as he continued to make me his bitch.

Couldn't wait until he was cumming inside of me. Or if he could make this last as long as possible, that would be great, too. The only problem with that was his wife finding out, but I was pretty sure she wasn't going to.

My fingers were digging hard into the bedsheets. He was pumping pleasure in my body with each hard, confident thrust of his. And I could feel he was getting closer to reaching his orgasm.

His beard looked perfect on him. I ran my hand through his short hair, noticing how sopping it was. Claude was more than 10 years older than me, and the fact he was betraying his wife with a gay guy like myself was telling.

She couldn't make him feel like the real man he was.

I couldn't stop stealing looks at his perfect body, noticing all the curves he had, the outlines, the shadows shifting as he used all of his muscles to keep eating me from behind.

His balls were still slapping off my ass and I could tell that he was still increasing his pace.

Claude was so big that he was stretching my rectum beyond everything I thought possible, hurting me as much as he was making me feel pleasure.

My moans were filling the room, even though my lips were shut and I was trying to contain them.

Just didn't want anybody finding out about what we were doing. If that happened, it would ruin something great we'd been building on for so long. So many months teasing him in his office and telling him about what he'd been missing...

Who could have known that all I needed was his wife snapping at him once and barking at him that he wasn't good enough for her? Had I known that, I'd have worked on that angle to make him come beg at my feet how much he needed me.

"Please don't stop. Don't you dare stop," I said through short breaths, realizing that pre-come was oozing from the tip of my much smaller cock. It couldn't even be compared to his.

Claude was nine inches long and who knew how thick. When I held his dong in my hand, all I could think about was that it was going to hurt me the first time he penetrated me.

Like it was happening now.

I moaned louder and more intensely than ever before, my body resonating with his when a shadow of something hit me in the face.

I shook my head, trying to understand what just happened and where that came from.

What the hell? I thought before realizing the door of the room was open. A ball of light was behind the shadow of a woman, who was standing in the doorway, glaring at us.

It was almost like she was thinking about killing us on the spot and damned be the consequences.

"Amelia?" Was the only thing that popped out of my mouth. My orgasm was ruined and even if this was nothing more than a nightmare, I didn't think I could go back into the mind space I was in.

"I knew something was up," she barked, striding into the room and yanking Claude off me.

Oh, no. This couldn't be happening. She was ruining the only fun thing still worth it in my life.

"I can explain everything," Claude exclaimed, lifting his hands over his head as he got on his knees. He was a tall and strong man.

The fact he was putting himself in that humiliating position was telling, as was the presence of Amelia in the room.

She had a pair of flip-flops, one that was still on her foot and the other that was on the other side of the room. Dressed as a pirate, she looked even more menacing than her usual self.

"Explain this, then," she said through gritted teeth. She lifted her hand, pointing a trembling finger at me. "You're telling me that you've been cheating on me with a *gay* guy? Should at least have had the decency of going for a woman. I feel humiliated."

He scrambled toward her, grabbing her ankles as he dove his head to her feet.

"It's my fault. I didn't tell him anything about us," he said and I could feel the fear in his voice. I kind of felt bad for him, but also, not that much.

I thought Claude was an experienced and confident man. I couldn't have been getting off on this if I hadn't been thinking that was the case.

"Get off me, you cheating cunt," she barked, slapping his face so hard he fell on the floor.

I bulged my eyes out. Something I didn't want to happen to me was her slapping me that hard, too. When she hurled that flip flop in my direction, it already hurt me so much.

I didn't know if I'd recover.

She stepped toward me and, as I was on my knees, I felt glued to the ground. I couldn't move. And whatever she was thinking about doing to me now, I knew that it couldn't be good at all.

"Now I need to figure out what to do with you. Can't let something like this slide," she said like she was doing everything in her power not to pull out a knife and kill me.

And even though I knew I didn't have to, I was choosing to go through with it. What better choice did I have?

CHAPTER 2

I handed over the document, my hand trembling. I didn't know what I was doing. I was in Amelia's house. In her office, to be more precise, and she had a smile on her face going from ear to ear.

I didn't know what was going on in her mind right now, but she had to be thinking that she 'got me.'

I was at her mercy now. She said she was going to transform me and turn me into a woman. I didn't think that was possible. Perhaps it was my curiosity speaking louder than my capability to think better about the things going on in my life, but… All I knew was that I couldn't go back on my word.

She wasn't using me, though. I was looking at this as a challenge. I didn't think she was going to be able to go through with it.

"Come. Follow me. I'm going to take you where you're needed," she said and I stood up. I followed her through a hallway. They had a big house. I didn't know where Claude was, but I was pretty sure he had to be nearby somewhere, most likely wondering how he could have fucked things up so badly.

She opened the door and I soon noticed that I was stepping into a bathroom. Stepping into a bathroom with the wife of the husband I was fucking? I wasn't going to deny I didn't think that was hot as balls, but my mind wasn't focusing on that.

Rather, I was focusing on getting through this alive.

"What are we doing here?" I asked as she closed the door.

"You're going to find out soon enough, honey," she said, turning on the showerhead. I raised an eyebrow. Was she going to make me watch her as she took a shower? If that was the case, it would be hot as fuck.

"I'm not going to do what you're thinking I am," she said, shaking her head as if she was reading my mind. She moved her hand up and down at me and added, "Strip. It's part of the process."

"What?" I asked, but she shook her head.

"Just take off your clothes."

Should I tell her I was bisexual? Before she noticed my hard and enraged cock, that was. Not that I thought she would think much of it, but still…

I took off my shirt, shorts, underwear, and everything else. I couldn't hide the heat rising to my cheeks, and it showed.

She watched the whole thing, including looking down at my dick and chuckling when she noticed that it wasn't very big.

"You're going to be perfect as a sissy," she said, walking until she was standing by the shower box. "Take a shower."

"Uhhh… what? I thought that you were going to turn me into a woman."

"Don't worry. It's going to happen soon enough."

I entered the shower box anyway, not even knowing if there were going to be clothes for me to change into later. The only thing that mattered now was not pissing her off any more.

I stepped under the water, letting it flow around my body as I soaped myself up. After throwing some shampoo on my hair and trying not to feel too hard that a hot woman was watching me, I walked out and toweled myself dry.

After tossing it into the hamper, I noticed that Amelia was still eyeing me with a finger on her bottom lip. Did she think I was hot or just that I was the perfect candidate she'd been looking for?

"Come. Follow me again. What we are going to do next can only be done in the other room," she explained, but my mind wasn't focused on her words. Rather, I was focusing on her swaying ass as she took me somewhere else in her house. It did look more like a mansion and I wasn't going to hide that from myself.

She opened the door and I noticed the single, raised bed in the middle of it. With piles of white towels and a cabinet full of pots, this looked more like a massage room.

But then my eyes noticed something else. Tape rolls, one on top of each other, on one of the sides of the room.

"Lie down on the bed. This won't take long and, take this," she said, her hand showing she was holding a pill. "It's for your transformation. I told you we're doing this seriously. You're never going back to becoming a man."

And if I could say no, that would be fine, too. That's what the agreement I signed said. But still... the prospect of becoming a woman for the rest of my life allured me. I'd been toying with the idea of going through that transformation one day, after all.

I took the pill and lied down on the bed. Amelia grabbed some pots, opened them, and then started to spread their creams over my skin.

I tried not to feel hard again. My libido was always high and I could fuck several women in a row without feeling gassed out.

Amelia smiled as she walked back to the rolls of tape. She grabbed one, proceeded back to me, and then put a length of it over the back of my thigh.

"So much hair. Gotta do something about this," she joked, yanking the tape off and making me feel pain as she removed all of my hair there.

I bit my bottom lip, already feeling better that I wasn't going to have any hair on my body other than on my head.

And the pill she gave me meant my dick was going to become so small I'd be able to cut it off later.

I wanted to become a complete woman, including having a pussy so that rough men like Claude could do whatever they wanted to me.

And I couldn't wait until I was seeing the end of this transformation.

CHAPTER 3

After applying and yanking several more lengths of tape, Amelia shaved off most of my hair. She had a look of happiness on her face, her smile going from ear to ear. I could almost read what she was thinking right now and how content she was for 'punishing me.'

She wasn't really doing that, though. In truth, I craved everything that was happening.

"Hop off the table. Time to shave off the rest of your body hair," she said, demanding that I go on with everything she was doing.

I jumped off the bed or table, or whatever it was called, my dick hard as she looked at it and said, "Can't wait until you don't have that thing anymore."

I didn't look at my dick with unhappiness. I couldn't wait until the pill did its thing and I could cut off my cock. It was everything I needed now.

Amelia pulled a chair and made me sit down on it. If there was one thing I wished she was doing now, it was getting naked for me. Knowing that wasn't going to happen, I decided not to focus on it.

She produced a scissor and a razor, getting on her knees in front of me. "This won't take long," she promised and I could tell she was right. It wasn't the first time she was shaving someone. No wonder Claude usually showed up without his chest and ass hair, even though I liked it.

I couldn't hide my boner and making my dick soft again was pretty much impossible. Amelia also didn't hold back every time she ended up touching my cock. She made the touches last long and they were also pretty sexy.

I couldn't wait for all the other things she had in store for me.

Not thinking about that much, I watched as she clipped off the hair on my nuts and ass. Amelia proceeded to shave them, making sure to slide the razor slowly and sensually. She didn't want to end up hurting me, and that was something I liked about her.

In the end, she still cared about me. But not because she looked at me knowing I was another human being like everyone else, but because she knew I needed to be well when I was transformed.

As time progressed, I noticed that my balls and cock were shrinking. Amelia didn't tell me anything about it, but I could tell that the pill had strong and immediate effects.

"Lift your arms," she said and I obeyed her. What other thing could I do now that wasn't that?

Spreading shaving foam on my armpits, she used the razor cautiously again. Before long, I felt like I'd been reborn. My skin was sensitive and I could feel the cool air swirling around me. It was a strange sensation.

"Now, it's time to put some makeup on you," she said, beckoning with her finger. This time, she took me to a bedroom.

Their bedroom. Still couldn't believe that I was walking into it again. I thought that, after she found out about what was happening, she was going to make this place forbidden for me.

"Sit down here," she asked and I did. I was sitting at the vanity as I looked at my naked self in front of the mirror. My eyes were showing my shock. I still couldn't wrap my head around all the things going on here.

Still couldn't believe that I wasn't going to be a man anymore after this.

"And since it's Halloween," I'm going to do something different for you, she said, picking up all the makeup items she was going to need. And those included the foundation, blush, lipstick, and pretty much everything else.

"What are you going to do that's so different?" I asked and she just laughed out loud.

"Oh, honey, you're soon going to find out," she responded as she put her hand on my eyes until I was closing them. "I'm going to make you look like a witch. You're a bitch and an asshole for having cheated on me with my husband. When I'm done with you, you won't even remember your old self."

I didn't say anything, hiding the smile that wanted to appear on my face. What if she noticed it and realized she actually needed to stop the transformation to truly punish me? If she did that, I'd be left defenseless and I'd feel like nothing in my life mattered anymore.

Amelia continued, grabbing brushes and other things she started to apply on my face. I was actually glad I wasn't seeing all the details of her applying the makeup on me. I wanted the result to be a surprise.

She stopped doing what she was doing. I fought back the urge to open my eyes, opting to wait until she put something on my head.

That came after she shaved off my head hair. I'd been so stupid when I thought she was already finished with me.

"Open your eyes, honey. Clothes will come later when you don't have your pathetic penis anymore," she said, putting a hand on my shoulder.

I opened my eyes and what I saw in front of me ceased to be the person I'd once been. She made me look like a witch, with rosy cheeks and pale-white skin.

Dark shades around my eyes made me look perfect for a Halloween party. I couldn't wait to go to another and make everyone think I was a woman.

"What do you think?" She asked and I could tell that if I said I didn't like it, she wouldn't hesitate to plunge a knife into my neck.

Not wanting to die quite yet, I answered, "It's lovely. When do you think my dick will fall off?"

"Soon, pretty soon, honey."

And as she finished saying that, I couldn't hide the excitement in me anymore. I smiled as I patiently waited for 'the putting clothes on me' part.

Couldn't wait to finish becoming a witch. Her witch.

CHAPTER 4

"What are you waiting for?" She asked, standing right on top of me. At the party, everyone thought I was a woman like everyone else. I knew it was wrong but it still felt so good. Almost as good as what she was doing to me now.

I was lying on the bed and Amelia was right on top of me. If she lowered her hips, she would be sitting on me. Instead, she was positioned in a way she was showing me her pussy. It was red and glistening with her orgasm.

"Your permission," I answered, knowing I couldn't go on without it. What if she thought I was stepping out of my boundaries? I couldn't let that happen, knowing that if I did, she would truly punish me.

It turned out that she knew everything that was going on in my mind during my transformation.

I lifted myself using my elbows, bringing my head closer to her cunt as I stuck my tongue out. The smell coming off of it was delicious and drool-inducing.

The only thing going on right now in my mind was how much I wanted to please her. And I couldn't believe that I was finally going to make that happen now.

When my tongue touched her pussy, it was like stars were exploding in my vision. Her juices were everything I thought they were going to be, making my cock strain against my cage.

To make her point clearer – that here in her house she called the shots - Amelia put a chastity cage on me. I hated it and I wanted to get it off right away, but I knew she wasn't going to budge.

I started to rub my tongue over her labia, enjoying every second of this. She threw her head backward, moaning and groaning as time passed. Sliding my tongue over her pussy was everything I thought it was going to be and a lot more, too.

"Faster, faster," she urged me on and I could only obey. My dick was oozing pre-cum and I couldn't stop noticing how small it had already gotten at this point.

It was still taking so long. I thought that, by now, it would already have reached the point of no return. It was a nice thing that I could still feel pleasure from it, though.

Amelia started to grind her pussy against my face and I couldn't help but think that this was anything but fair. She was the only one having the orgasm of her life.

Amelia continued to grind her pussy over my face until she was moaning so loudly I knew the neighbors were hearing everything. They were probably all thinking it was Claude the one making her feel happier than she'd ever been.

If only they knew, I thought with an amused smile on my face.

Her body was slick with sweat, drops rivuleting down her body as she started to calm down. Amelia looked down, noticing that I was still underneath her.

At some point, she must have forgotten about me. No wonder she was looking at me now with surprise in her eyes.

"I'm far from done with you, honey," she commented, moving her fingers through the strands of my wig. She said that I couldn't grow my hair naturally, which was disappointing. I wanted to find out what it looked like when it was long.

Not thinking about that much more, I focused on calming down my breathing. It was such a shame that she wasn't going to please me any more. And I loved licking her pussy, too.

"Time for the final act," she revealed and I was giggling. I couldn't wait until she was taking the virginity of my ass, too. She took the V-card of my mouth and that was an experience like no other.

Taking in a deep breath, she grabbed a strap-on and put it on her hips.

"Turn around," she said and I obeyed. It was the only thing that could be done.

Her hands started to slide over my buttcheeks, feeling and kneading them. There was no denying that the only thought in her mind now was shoving that thing deep inside of me, I remembered.

"Please don't hurt me much."

Amelia stopped sliding her hands, pressing her fingers into my skin. I couldn't see her face, but I could tell she was smiling. Why did I even think that asking anything of her was going to change her mind?

"Not going to happen, and it's not like you really want that," she said, grabbing my hair with one hand and yanking me to her with force.

I felt her strap-on breaking through the first barrier, penetrating me and then going in all the way. She reached the end of my rectum in a fraction of a second, pounding in and out of me right away.

She was relentless. Never before had I felt so much pain and pleasure. I was moaning and groaning with Amelia, announcing to everyone in the block that I was going to start living with her. I couldn't see myself moving out of here and I could tell that she shared the same thoughts.

I didn't know how her strap-on worked, but I was already cumming in my chastity cage as she climaxed with me. Her moans were almost impossible to ignore.

Moments later, Amelia stopped and pulled out of me. The strap-on was looking a little slick and dirty after our fuck, and she tossed it away like it didn't mean anything to her.

She jumped off the bed, throwing on some clothes as if she was getting ready for a party.

I blinked twice when I noticed a shadow standing in the doorway. It was Claude, who was linking his arm with his wife. They were going to a Halloween party and I wasn't going along with them.

And frankly, the only thing I was surprised about was that she forgave him, in the end.

GENDER SWAPPING MY MAID HUSBAND

A First Time Sissification Halloween Story

CHAPTER 1

"So, what are you going to do now?" She asked, making me realize I couldn't say no. She was my wife and, as such, I had to do pretty much everything she asked. My whole life, I'd always been a very submissive husband. And I didn't think that could ever be changed.

She was pointing her trembling finger at me. I could only wonder what was going on in her mind right now.

My friends had already told me I needed to stand up for myself, but little did they know that doing so was harder than they thought.

"Everything you want from me," I responded, feeling my cock twitching in my pants. It had been a long time since we last made love. I wanted to do everything she wanted from me, but that was more difficult than I thought.

"Everything I want from you?" She asked, leaning down and making me wonder if she was going to kiss me.

My wife was one of the most beautiful women in the world and she had every right to be thinking she had control over me.

She had, after all.

"Everything you want," I responded, knowing I was making a mistake, but going through with it anyway.

What else was I going to do? My life with her had always been like this - me doing everything she wanted.

She put her hand on my lap, moving it up and making me wonder if she was going to start touching my bulge. It was hard and growing, and I was only wondering if she was going to let me come inside her again.

"Anything I want?" She asked, leaning down again and showing me what she was hiding under her shirt.

Her breasts. I couldn't stop thinking about them, already licking my lips. Amelia smiled.

She knew she was the one on top and she wasn't going to hide that. If anything, she was going to keep using that in her favor.

"I like the sound of that," I said, putting my hand on her thigh, sliding it up along with her dress. She had a skimpy one-piece on, and it was barely enough to cover her body.

I should be raging that she went to work today wearing that, but I couldn't. I loved how slutty she could be sometimes.

Her skin was incredibly soft, I thought as I moved my hand further up until I was mere inches from finding her fanny.

Amelia locked her eyes with me, telling me a million things through them. Alright. I was going to do what she wanted.

Kneading her skin, I asked, "So, what's that going to entail? You can't keep me in the dark. I won't allow it."

She leaned down even more, putting her lips close to my ear. "I'll give you a pill and you will become a woman."

Become a woman? Call me crazy, but I didn't think she was in her right state of mind.

I just didn't think doing that was even possible. It felt like she was coming up with something that didn't exist.

"I don't believe you."

"You don't? Don't you remember what happened to Derrick? You were cheating on me with him and look at what happened to him. Do you think there won't be any consequences for you too?"

It was like I was having a bad case of amnesia. She was right. She did those things to Derrick and now he lived with us, being her sex servant.

"I was thinking we needed a maid and I can't trust someone from the outside. That's why I was thinking about turning you into one," she said, moving her legs and sitting on me. I could feel her cunt against my hardening cock, and it was such a pity we couldn't do anything right now. Amelia wouldn't allow it.

I gulped. "I'm not sure I'm ready to do something like that…"

"What are you saying? You've always been a womanizer and you think you can fuck any woman in the world. I can't keep ignoring that."

She breathed long on my neck, feeling what I smelled like. Goosebumps across my arms, and I was already wondering what I was thinking by defying her - even if only slightly. "And then I'll also invite a friend."

I should be submitting myself completely to her, I thought.

"What friend? Oh, don't you tell me you've been cheating on me too this whole time."

"No, nothing like that," she responded, sliding her hand over my leg, finding my bulge, and pressing on it.

She was relentless. She was making me so hard I was already leaking pre-come, and the smell of it was rising in the air.

Amelia had me where she wanted. She was hot. She was over-confident. Her smile was beautiful and brighter than I thought a woman's smile could ever be.

She pressed her lips to mine and I also felt her bust pressing against my hard muscles. I worked out. I kept myself in shape. It was all for her and my other partners.

It was such a nice surprise that she was still keeping me with her. I thought that, by now, she'd already have dumped me.

"So, what do you say? Are you going to take the pill and become my maid?" She asked, connecting her lips to mine again, and it was such a wet kiss that a line of saliva still kept us connected when she moved her head back slightly.

"Everything you want. Just like I promised," I answered and I knew I was making a decision I couldn't go back on.

I was going to become her sissy maid. Maid husband. Husband maid or whatever she wanted to call it. The important thing now was keeping in mind I couldn't go back on it.

And I couldn't wait until she presented her friend to me, too.

CHAPTER 2

I pulled the thong, loving how it felt and looked on me. I was in front of a large body-sized mirror, checking myself out. The room was silent, even though I could hear the beating of music not too far from me.

Still couldn't believe that I was now working as a sissy maid, but beggars couldn't be choosers, I thought. That's what I kept in mind right now.

I was and looked like a sissy maid, a tiara on my head shining under the soft light of the lamp hanging from the ceiling. But I also looked like a witch and the makeup that my wife applied on me even made me look like that. That's why I was proud of myself.

The first day after the transformation, I still couldn't believe how much I changed. My breasts were bigger than I thought they were going to be.

My cock and balls fell off. I still had more muscles than a woman should have, but anyone looking at me now would think I was female. There was no denying that.

The door opened, my wife stepping through it. I didn't know what costume she wore, but it was a pretty skimpy one. I could see most of her body, including the color of her thong.

Now that she turned me into a sissy, she couldn't stop hiding how pleased she was at how everything turned out. Her smile was going from ear to ear.

"Love your new look," she said, approaching me from behind and putting a hand on my belly. I was still taller than her, but she didn't let that distract her. If anything, it seemed to turn her on even more.

She moved her hand down, sneaking it under my witch dress. Finding my clit, she started to press it.

My cock fell off and then that pretty little clit appeared. It was the most sensitive part of my body.

"I love this part of yours. I keep thinking about it," she purred, starting to rub her finger on it, making me feel all sorts of things.

"Let me please you. Let me worship you," I said and that widened her smile.

"I've been thinking about letting you do that. You're such a slut," she said, taking off the wings on her back.

I still didn't know what her costume was. It looked like that of an angel or butterfly. I was so bad at figuring out this kind of thing.

"I'm your slut, and I'm already wondering what your friend really looks like. I want him to fuck me when he's ready."

"Oh, honey. He's always ready," she said, rubbing my clit a little more and then sliding her finger down. I locked my eyes with her when she did something I didn't think she had the guts for.

She scooped up some of my pussy juice, lifting her hand and then licking it with her tongue. I looked at that while wondering what was going on in her mind.

I just never thought it was possible.

"There's a lot more where that came from," she said, taking my hand and walking with me to the bed.

I didn't have to ask her what she wanted to do right now. She lifted her legs, putting them over my shoulders.

I was still mesmerized by the softness of her skin. My fingers couldn't stop pressing into it, kneading it like it was the last thing I was doing with my life.

She grabbed the hem of her dress, pulling it up and showing me what she was hiding under there.

Amelia also wore a thong, and it had a large wet spot on it. This whole time, she'd been more excited than she should be.

"Worship me. Make me feel that you're worth it," she said, and I leaned down and did what she asked of me. I stuck my tongue out and took in a deep breath, loving the patch of hair on her cunt.

It was just like I remembered it. She wasn't the kind of woman that liked shaving, and it showed.

Amelia locked her eyes with me, moving her head back when she felt my tongue touching her cunt again. And I let it there, just pressing against it, not thinking about anything else right now.

I started to move it up and down, rubbing over it and loving the taste of her cunt juice. I opened my eyes and noticed that her fanny was quivering, trembling, and needing more of me.

At the end of the day, there was no one quite like me when it came to pleasing her. That's why she needed me to be doing this.

And then I would have what I'd been waiting for this whole time. Pleasing her friend and finding out what she'd been hiding from me this whole time.

I kept pressing my fingers into the skin of her thighs, licking her cunt, loving her taste, wondering if one day she could do the same to me, now that I also had something that looked just like hers.

The only difference was that I shaved every day. I couldn't go a day without doing that.

She was moaning, louder than ever before, and I could only keep licking her cunt, using my fingers to give her additional pleasure, and her body was resonating with me.

She started to squirm and convulse, and I was so wet I was sweating all over my body.

Amelia was moaning so loudly that there was no way nobody in the house was hearing that.

Oh, they were hearing everything alright and they couldn't do anything about it.

I needed to find out who her friend was and, considering the type of woman Amelia was, I knew that he had to be one of the biggest in the city.

I couldn't wait to find out what he could do to me when he was in one of the rooms, pleasing me.

And Derrick? He could join in and help us with doing everything else. He could help with cleaning up after us when we were done.

Amelia stopped squirming, sliding her legs off my body and lighting up a cigarette.

She was done with me and I knew it was time to find out what the Halloween party had in store for me.

My heart was thumping in my chest and I knew that, whatever that was, it had to be good.

CHAPTER 3

I walked to the door, not surprised when I found out that a huge black guy was ripping off the shirt that Derrick wore.

She was on her knees on the bed, trying to dig into the bedsheets like it was the last thing she was doing with her life.

Now that Derrick was a woman, using female pronouns felt right and was the right thing to do.

Derrick also had a different name now. She was called Erica, which was such a pretty name I was already wondering when I was going to be given my new name, too.

Erica turned her head to look at me, her wide eyes telling me that she was surprised I was here.

She didn't need to be, though. When my former wife told me that I was going to find my surprise here, I came as quickly as I could.

And I smiled when I saw what that surprise was. A huge black man, bigger than I thought a man could ever be.

He was naked and I could see his whole body, my eyes darting down and finding his big cock, beads of pre-come seeping out of the slit.

"I'm Bayden, if you want to know my name," he said, ignoring Erica and making a beeline to me as he showed that his intention was just one. Claiming me in ways I never thought possible.

To rip off my costume and to show me that he wasn't the kind of man that played with his food.

"I don't think that's necessary," I said, watching as he loomed toward me, looking bigger with each step he took.

He grabbed my arms and pushed me up against the wall, his fingers digging deep, hurting me and not stopping even though he knew.

He lowered his head, smelling me. It was such a weird sensation what I was feeling, finally feeling my pussy as it got wetter.

"I love the smell of a woman like you," he said, taking one hand off my forearm and moving it down over the curves of my body.

He had a very big hand, so big that it was making me feel smaller than I already was.

And I loved everything about him. The room was dark and I could see all the curves and the lines that defined his body, his scent unlike anything I'd smelled before.

If I still had a cock, I would be hard right now. Instead, I was wet and, on top of that, I was desperate for him to penetrate me.

I could only wonder what he would make me feel when he was inside of me.

He put his tongue out and started to lick my skin, making sure that he was tracing the curves of my neck.

I squirmed and melted in his presence, putting my hands on his shoulders and feeling the hardness of his muscles. Bayden looked a lot older than me, but his skin was still very soft.

Veins bulging in his arms caught my attention, his hands moving, going up and down, sliding over my skin, feeling every inch of me.

I moaned when he moved a finger down and found my pussy, pressing a finger to my labia.

He locked his eyes with me when he said, "I found your honey-pot."

He opened a smile as he said that, loving every second of the action he was having with me.

I didn't try to fight back, surprised when he let go of me and allowed me to get on my knees on the floor.

I turned my head to the left when I realized that Erica was still here with us, fingering herself as she watched everything that was happening.

She had the best view and I kind of envied her, though not very long.

I turned my eyes back to the right when I noticed the big cock that he had, knowing that it was almost ten inches in length.

I licked my lips as I felt like I was born to be a slut, my heart pounding in my chest.

He wrapped his fingers around his cock as he pushed it down, making me see that it was pointed right to my mouth. I took a deep breath in as I realized I was going to have a cock just for myself for the first time in my life.

All the times I had sex with a guy, they always bottomed for me. I always thought, my entire life, I was only a top, but now I knew different. Now I knew better.

I wrapped my lips around his cock, knowing that I made the best decision of my life when I decided to become a woman.

In the first few seconds, I put only a few inches of his cock in my mouth. If I put too much of it at once, I knew that I wouldn't be able to do this the way it was supposed to be done.

Bayden was already rock-hard the moment I put his shaft in my mouth, and as I started to work it, moving my head up and down, I knew that it wasn't going to take him long until he was coming in my mouth.

And I couldn't wait to find out what he tasted like.

Minutes later, he started to unload his sperm down my throat, rewarding me with the salty taste of his release.

His pumping didn't stop until after about two minutes, and he had so much of it that I felt, at some point, he wasn't going to stop and was going to kill me by overfeeding my belly.

I breathed out a sigh of relief when that didn't happen, Bayden pulling out of my mouth and petting my head.

"We'll meet again sometime," he said, walking out of the room dressed after putting on his ghost costume.

Knowing the number of people dressed just like him, I knew that finding him was going to be impossible.

And not focusing on that much, I turned my head to the left. Erica was still experimenting with her cunt, and it was time for her to teach me what she already knew about it.

She opened a smile, and I knew she wanted me as much as I wanted her.

CHAPTER 4

"**L**ooks like someone's already waiting for me," I said, climbing up on the bed and putting my hand under her.

She looked at me, putting a finger on her lips as she asked me to turn her around. No point in pretending that I didn't come here to do this, so I obeyed her.

She lifted her rear, pointing it right at me. I took in a deep breath, looking at how beautiful and lust-inducing it was.

I could keep admiring it like this for hours if I didn't have something better to do.

I didn't focus on that much, instead opting to lower my head and lick her fanny. That wasn't enough for me, and so I moved my hand and pressed my fingers to her labia.

"How does it feel like to finally have a cunt? Is it something that you've always been looking for?" I asked, pressing my lips to her asscheeks.

They were soft, perfect, and very succulent. I could go for hours with my lips pressed to her ass like this, and I knew that Erica would enjoy that, too.

Meanwhile, the party was still raging outside. People were having a lot of fun in my house.

When it was my time to go down there, I'd like to be their maid and show them what I could do.

I knew the party was populated with guys as open-minded as I was. And the women, too...

I knew they wouldn't think twice before getting behind me

with their strap-ons and fucking me until nothing was left.

I couldn't wait until that happened. Was that going to take too long? I didn't think so.

Returning my attention to the sissy underneath me, I gave her cunt a couple more confident licks before moving my arms around her.

It was time to find her breasts and do to them everything she was thinking I could do.

Pressing my fingers against them, she moaned as she thrust her hips against me.

"Oh, calm down there. I'm not even started with you yet," I said, keeping my voice low as I focused my attention on her.

"Please don't hurt me much," she said, and I could only smile at that. It was just like her to say something like that.

"I'll think about it," I said, pressing my fingers into the skin of her boobs one more time, and then putting two fingers on her nipples.

She turned her head so that she was looking into my eyes and I could see that she was begging for me not to do what I had in mind.

I chuckled as I squeezed her nipples and made her moan so hard I thought she was going to pass out.

Seconds later, I was happy she didn't. No fun in fucking her if she didn't know what was happening.

I lowered my head and licked her pussy a couple more times, loving the sweat drops on her skin. I could tell that Erica was afraid of what I could do to her.

Not thinking anymore and focusing on all the things that I was going to make her feel, I reached outside the bed and picked up a strap-on. It was just lying on the floor, pleading for me to put it on me.

And I did that, taking in the view of this newly born woman underneath me. I couldn't fuck her with my old cock and, to be honest, I wouldn't try doing that even if I could.

All I wanted was to feel like a woman. And to do that, sometimes it meant going through the same disadvantages that a woman had.

"I'm going to make this extra-special to you," I murmured into her ear, pressing my hard-on to her asshole, breaking through the first barrier and stopping only when I was so deep that I couldn't see anything other than the band of my strap-on.

Erica groaned and moaned, pressing the walls of her rectum around the rubber toy that was filling her.

I stayed inside of her for the first few seconds, letting her feel my weight and size.

The weight and size of my strap-on, I thought to myself. A very important distinction that I needed to keep in mind.

And thinking about something else, I couldn't wait until my ex-wife fucked me again with a strap-on. Nothing quite like being the submissive husband that I'd always been.

I started to roll my hips, pounding against her ass like this was the last thing I was doing with my life.

The pleasure that I was feeling, that sensation that my orgasm was coming and that it was going to roll through me like nothing before it… It was all there and I couldn't control it.

And in less than a few seconds, it came and if there was something I was wishing was happening now, it was coming inside of Erica too. Instead, all I got was an orgasm like no other in my life, my cunt dripping wet on the bedsheets.

I pulled out of her, panting and knowing that soon I was going to make the whole party fuck me too.

I couldn't wait until I became their slut on Halloween.

GENDER SWAPPED AND REGRESSED

*A First Time Sissification
Halloween Story*

CHAPTER 1

I cracked open my eyes, feeling something odd on my hips. I looked down and sighed. I couldn't believe that she put another chastity device on me! Must have been because, last night, I figured a way to take it off without breaking it.

I was thinking about putting it back on soon. Amelia was a hard-to-please Mistress. If she didn't have everything her way, she'd punish me. And now, she was punishing me again.

Couldn't believe that, to make all of this happen, all I needed to do was to cheat with her husband.

Her husband, who was now also a sissy. Couldn't believe all the things we went through, I thought.

I sat up on the bed and squinted my eyes. I was looking around in the room, trying to figure out if it was still the same place or not. Something was telling me that it wasn't, though.

No lights in the room, no nothing other than the bed I was seated on.

I pushed the comforter off me, feeling the weight of the chastity cage.

This one was made of metal and I could tell that the locking mechanism was a lot tougher than the previous one. Tampering with this one wasn't going to be easy at all.

I groped the hard, metal material for a moment when the door opened. A beautiful, slender figure was thrown into the room, and a large and menacing woman was behind her.

With her other hand, she was holding a whip. I gulped. I didn't think that my punishment was going to come so soon. I thought

I'd have a lot more time.

As I looked down again, I realized that the person thrown into the room was none other than Claude.

Wow... I still couldn't believe the sort of things she made me feel the other night.

That's why Amelia was looking so pissed off right now. We shouldn't have touched each other. She couldn't control Bayden, though.

He just shrugged his shoulders and walked out of the house when she complained.

Now that I was thinking about it, I couldn't wait until he came back. His cock was just so big!

I put my hands up in front of me.

"Wait, what do you think you're doing?" I asked when she closed the door. The room fell into a layer of complete darkness, and I could see nothing around me.

Nothing other than the eyes of the two people still here with me.

A finger flipped up a switch and a bulb flashed to life in the room. Amelia was dressed the part.

A harness pressed around her body, showing me all of her nice curves. Red lipstick, hair pinned up, skin looking slick – like she'd spread some kind of lotion on her body.

I wondered what happened, and I didn't have much time to be wondering about that kind of thing, I soon noticed.

"You didn't think I didn't know what was happening this whole time?" She asked, making a beeline to me.

My legs scrambled as I tried to move away from her, losing my footing and falling over on the floor.

"Wait, I didn't mean to do what I did. I tried to stop Claude, but she didn't listen. She wouldn't listen."

She was still looming in front of me when I gasped. I thought that, for sure, she was going to lift her whip and start to strike me with it, but she stopped.

Amelia smiled as she said, "I believe you. For the first time in my life, I believe you."

I widened my eyes as I jumped to her, grabbing her ankles. I shot my head up, looking at her face and asking for her forgiveness.

"Please don't punish me, Mistress. I know you don't want to do that."

"I'm thinking about that," she said, shaking her legs as she forced me to let go of them. I always knew that was going to happen, and I always knew that asking for her forgiveness was a mistake.

I just needed to do that, though.

Claude was getting back on her feet, blinking several times in a row.

"What's happening here?" She asked, taking a step forward when she realized she wasn't alone. She realized that she wasn't just with her, but also with me.

"I have a surprise for you two," Amelia said, producing a pacifier in her hand. It was blue, made of plastic and rubber, and the backside of it had a doodle on it. It looked pretty and also big enough for an adult.

I wasn't stupid, I thought as I realized what was going on here. Age regression. She was going to turn me into a little.

I'd read about that so many times before, and I never thought it would happen to me one day.

"What's that?" Claude asked, making me realize that we hadn't chosen a proper name for her sissy self yet. I wondered if that was going to happen at the end of this.

Not wanting to do anything that might piss Amelia off, I decided to make no questions about that right now.

"It looks like someone in the room has already understood what's happening. I'm sorry, sissy Claude, but you've always been a very stupid man. Turning you into a sissy didn't change anything."

"I don't get it," she said, still blinking her eyes and looking as stupid as before.

Amelia waved her hand. "Oh, don't worry about that. I'm going to explain everything," she said, looking from me to her.

She took a deep breath in, letting a moment of pause settle in the room. It was empty and I didn't think it was going to remain like that for very long.

Something was telling me that she was going to be bringing new things into the room very soon.

"You're going to become my littles. I'm going to completely, utterly own you. Your lives will be even more different. You'll wear diapers, be allowed to crawl around only, and sleep in the cribs. It's going to be incredible and I'm sure you're going to love it."

And hearing that, Claude shut her eyes and fell on the floor. Wow. I didn't think that was going to happen.

Now that she knew what was going to happen, she passed out.

CHAPTER 2

Claude woke up moments later, looking at me and then at my chastity cage. She was lying on the floor and Amelia was seated on the bed. She was still holding the whip, most likely thinking about the best ways to use it.

She produced another paci, grabbing her arm and then yanking her. "Open your mouth," Amelia demanded and she obeyed. From husband to sissy and now to little. I couldn't wrap my head around the humiliation she was going through.

After shoving the pacifier into her mouth, I thought she was going to spit it out. She didn't, looking at me while Amelia checked her out.

"I really thought you were a real man. Looks like I'm going to need Bayden again," she murmured, opening a smile on her face.

Claude didn't say anything. She just stood where she was, blinking like she couldn't believe the turn of events that changed her life.

"And look, your name from now on is going to be Julia. Sorry, I couldn't come up with a different one," Amelia chuckled, making me feel a crack of hatred for her.

She was humiliating her more than I thought someone could without feeling abhorred by it. Amelia ceased being a human a long time ago.

"Lie down on the floor, Julia. My bladder is full," she demanded of her and I thought she wasn't going to obey.

After all, it was going beyond everything and anything I thought okay for a moment like this one.

She lied on the floor, moving her hand and attempting to take off her pacifier. But Amelia swatted it and stopped her before she could make that mistake.

"No, that's going to remain there. You are not allowed to take off your paci for the time being. I want it there while I'm pissing on your face," she said, opening a smile.

Claude didn't widen her eyes like I thought she was going to. Instead, she pulled the corners of her lips as Amelia approached her, squatting above her.

She pulled down her thong, a stream of yellow liquid coming out of her asshole.

It hit Julia's face, splashing all over it as she closed her eyes. I breathed a sigh of relief when I noticed that she did that. I thought that she was going to get blinded by the piss.

Amelia remained where she was, looking down at Julia with that same smile on her face.

I knew she was going to take pleasure in the humiliation she was inflicting on her sissy, but what was happening here was way more than that.

Julia reopened her eyes, blinking rapidly.

"And one more thing," Amelia said, lowering her hands and groping her boobs. "You're also not allowed to say anything. If you do, you will get punished even harder."

I gulped. I knew this was going to be hard for me, but I didn't think she was going to forbid me from speaking.

Amelia produced another pacifier and I opened my mouth at the same moment. I knew what she was going to do and I got ready for it.

She shoved the pacifier into my mouth and, for a moment, I thought I wasn't going to like it. But then my tongue touched the teat and I pressed my lips around it, and I thought that… It was actually good.

Amelia lifted her hand, putting it on my head. She rubbed my forehead as she widened her smile. I knew she was going to do that and that I was going to like it.

My whole life, I'd always dreamed of being put back in my

place.

The smell of her piss was still in the air, impregnating it. I thought I wasn't going to like it, but now I did. I wanted her to piss on me, too.

She lowered her hand, putting it on my shoulder.

"Lie down on the bed. I'm going to do something special with you, too."

And I could only obey her, looking up at the bright light hanging from the ceiling.

"You've always been such a submissive sissy. I knew I was going to enjoy this when I transformed you, but I never thought it was going to be like this."

With the pacifier in my mouth, I couldn't speak even if I wanted to.

Amelia climbed up on the bed, putting herself on top of me. I checked her out from top to bottom, loving the curves and lines that defined her body.

It was like she was a goddess and I was just her servant. Her obedient, submissive sissy that had once been a man...

And now she was regressing me and turning me into her little. First, inflicting pain on me and making me feel that I needed everything she had, including her piss and even her...

A slab of feces came out of her hole, falling onto my boobs. And then came another and one more. I was staring at her wide-eyed.

I did know about the pissing-on-us part, but I didn't think she was also going to poop, too.

What the hell was even going on in her mind right now? I couldn't even try to read it.

Oh, and the smell of it too. Terrible, but also... There was something about it I was enjoying. I was feeling so humiliated I didn't think I'd ever come back from this.

And she lowered her right hand, pressing it on my feces and spreading it over my breasts.

"Oh, look what a mess this is. Seems that someone needs a shower now."

CHAPTER 3

"Hmm, I love doing this," she said, lifting her legs and putting them on my back. I was kneeling on the floor, on all fours, and she was using me as a leg rest.

The humiliation she was making me feel was hardening my nipples. They were so hard right now I couldn't hide that even if I was trying to.

And to make everything worse – or better – she was also having dinner.

Dressed as a pirate, she looked even scarier now. Around us were all the people that weren't going to remember an ounce of this once it was over.

They might remember that someone who looked like me had been here, but they'd just brush that off and pretend it was nothing more than a curious memory.

"I love being your submissive sissy," I said, looking up and noticing that Julia was lowering her head.

Her hand settled on the underside of her boob, pushing it up while she guided Amelia's nipple into her mouth.

She pressed her lips around it tentatively, knowing that this was the first time she was doing that. If she pissed Amelia off, she'd be in a bad spot.

Her skin looked slick with her sweat, almost like she'd spread oil all over it.

Amelia lifted her hand, putting it on her head as she said.

"You're doing well, Julia. Don't worry. Just keep this up and you're going to be fine."

Julia's eyes were trembling. Before this, she was a man and would be the one calling the shots. Now, everything changed.

"Thanks, Mistress," she said, her voice sounding more and more feminine. I didn't know anything about the pill Amelia used, but it was pretty good.

It was changing everything about our pasts, and I couldn't even remember anymore what we'd been like before.

Not all the details anymore, I thought.

"No need to thank me. Actually, I don't want you to do that. Just keep working on that nipple, Julia."

Julia's eyes flashed like she now knew everything she needed to be doing to keep pleasing her ex-wife.

Dammit. I couldn't let her win. I didn't know if this was a competition without Amelia telling me anything about that, but I wasn't the kind of woman that liked losing.

Julia took her lips off the nipple and reached over for the other. She pressed her small fingers in, letting them disappear in the skin of Amelia's huge breast.

Even though I wasn't the one doing the touching, I couldn't deny that it looked heavy.

I licked my lips as I drooled. I couldn't wait until I was the one doing the same.

I couldn't stop feeling the ball of coldness on my back. It was coming from the platter Amelia had put on it.

She was picking grapes and fruit pieces from it, watching a horror movie on TV.

Around us, guests stumbled and bumped against each other, drunker than they'd ever been.

The stench of cigarettes in the air couldn't be ignored and it was one of the few things about the party I wished was different. Nothing that could be done about it, though.

Amelia patted my shoulder, reaching down and pressing her hand to one of my boobs.

"Hmmm… it's growing and becoming better than ever. You're not looking so bad yourself. Any of these days I'll let you walk out and find a man that wants to marry you."

"Marry me?" I asked, not believing what she was saying. "But I don't want to marry. I want to live here for the rest of my life and serve you, Mistress."

She chuckled, putting one leg on top of the other.

"I knew you were going to say that."

She retreated her hand, lowering it to her pussy. It was glistening under the soft glow of the ceiling lamps. Someone brushed against her shoulder and she kicked him so hard he fell over on the floor.

I scowled at him and he scrambled away. Wearing a mask, I didn't even know who he was and didn't care.

The only thing that mattered now was pleasing Amelia and showing her I was the only one she needed.

"Fucking hell. Where's Bayden when I need him?" She asked, turning her head from side to side while a mist surrounded us.

Everything was so dark and the mist was making it look even more opaque.

As if on cue, he appeared out of nowhere, holding his massive, ten inches long cock and guiding it into her mouth.

She wrapped her fingers around it and I noticed that she couldn't fully enclose his girth.

Holy damn. I knew he was big, but I didn't think he was that big. It was like he was an alien.

"This is what I've been waiting for," she said, sliding the shaft deeper into her mouth. So deeper I was wondering how she wasn't gagging and coughing right now.

She was taking it all in like this wasn't the first time she was doing that with him.

She pressed her lips around it and I noticed that Bayden was still dressed like an African soldier.

A mighty warrior that knocked up several women and populated entire cities, I joked. Or was that really a joke? It could be that it was real and I didn't know anything about it.

Shivering, I watched in astonishment as Amelia bobbed up and down on him. Her lips were so stretched I could see white lines appearing.

Amelia picked up the pace, going up and down faster and harder. His balls tightened up as he took his cock out of her mouth.

"Fuck, you always make me come so fast," he growled, his massive rod throbbing while he unloaded rope after rope of his sperm all over her face.

He was painting it white and, for a moment, I wished he was doing that to me. I wished he was also knocking me up and I could have his heirs.

Maybe sometime later, I thought. They had so many things prepared for us, after all.

CHAPTER 4

Amelia sat on the bed, smirking at me. "Come on. I'm going to let you please me for a little while," she said, and I could feel the diaper pressing against my hips and butt.

She put it on me a long time ago and hadn't mentioned anything about me taking a shower, too. Now that I was thinking about it, I didn't think she was going to do it.

I approached her, noticing that I was on my knees. I couldn't walk like any other person anymore.

She didn't allow it, and I wouldn't change that about my life even if I could.

I loved being her submissive sissy.

I moved a little closer to her, standing no more than some inches from her pussy. It was still glistening under the soft glow of a lamp.

She lowered her hand, pulling one of her pussy lips to the side.

I licked my lips and put my tongue out. My heart was hammering in my chest when I lowered my head. I touched the lower side of her cunt, imagining making her come all over my face.

I knew she would like that.

I gave her cunt several licks in a row, loving her taste. She put a hand on my forehead and made me stop. I blinked twice, not understanding why she was doing that.

"It's delicious. Why did you make me stop?"

"Well, you can't have everything in one go," she explained and I could see where she was coming from.

Still, I looked down and checked out her snatch again.

Nothing quite like it, her legs spread open, her skin looking slick and smooth.

I put my hands on her legs, moving them up and down.

"Don't stop doing that. I love your technique," she moaned and that made me feel more thrilled to go on.

Taking a hand off her leg, I slid a finger inside her tunnel. She bucked her hips and, for a moment, I thought she was going to come for sure.

With that not happening, I slid another finger into her fanny. It felt tight and so warm, and also pretty wet.

I couldn't imagine myself taking my finger out of there any-time soon.

Not until she told me the magical words, I reminded myself.

"Lick it again. Make me come. Make me happy," she said and my heart sped up. She didn't need to ask me again to do that.

I lowered my head again, nearing her pussy and diving deeper between her legs.

I smelled the scent of her cunt, and it was driving me crazy. This was it - the moment I'd been waiting for.

I moved my other hand to her intimate parts, this time looking for her clit. It was hard and enraged, like a little nub that just couldn't be sated. I smiled, giving her labia more strong and confident licks.

And the way she was squirming on the bed was driving me crazier. I moaned, realizing that I couldn't finger myself. The chastity cage and the diaper were in the way.

Not that I could do that anyway, thanks to my hands being already too busy with Amelia. Her eyes closed, she was groaning louder than my slurping and gobbling noises.

I didn't know where this was going to lead, but I was sealing my life with her. I was never going to turn back and return to being the person I'd once been.

Giving her pussy more wide and long licks, I loved the taste of her cunt. My finger was rubbing her bundle of nerves, driving her to think that she was going to pass out. I didn't want this moment to stop.

"Oh, fuck, fuck, fuck," she said, her body emanating heat in the air. I kept fingering her, more often than not pressing my fingers on her rosebud as I knew she was getting close to orgasming.

It was going to happen-

It did, her juices pouring all over my face. And even then, I didn't stop fingering and licking her pussy lips. In fact, I'd say that Amelia reaching her climax was making it all the better for me.

I was coming too, smearing milk all over the interior of my diaper. Mistress was going to be pissed.

She'd said that I couldn't do that and I'd agreed with her. Punishment was going to be severe, but I didn't mind it.

A moment later, she stopped squirming, her breathing slowing down as she reopened her eyes.

Amelia smiled and picked up her cigarette pack. She fished one out and lit it up using a lighter.

She put the lighter back on the nightstand, blowing smoke through her nostrils.

"You didn't come, or did you? I said that you couldn't," she said, keeping a smile on her face as if to tell me she knew everything going on in my mind.

Even lying to her now was going to be difficult, I thought. Not that I could do that before without getting caught red-handed, though.

I let a tear come out and roll down my cheek. She gave me a knowing look and put her cigarette in the ashtray.

Then, she stood up and walked to a point in the room.

Picking up something, she turned around and showed it to me. It was a collar with a leash, and my name was on it.

"Whether you came or not doesn't really matter. You were going to be punished either way," she said, walking over to me and putting the collar around my neck.

When she snapped it close, I knew that she was telling me the truth.

And I was thrilled that I wasn't just going to be her sissy and plaything, but also her pet now.

SISSY BREACHED BY BBC ON HALLOWEEN

*A Gender Swap Male
to Female Story*

CHAPTER 1

"You've lost the game!" Amelia said, grinning from ear to ear. My heart skipped a beat. I couldn't believe that I lost a game and that now I was going to have to do whatever they wanted with me. I had no idea what they had in store for me.

Seated across from me was a huge, black man that didn't partake in the game. He was much bigger than me, easily standing more than 6 foot five.

Even though he was seated and so was I, I could tell that if he was standing right in front of me, that my eyes would be where his shoulders were.

When Amelia announced that I lost the game, he turned his eyes to look at me. It was like he was telling me a million things through them, and not a single one of them was good for me. He was already preparing all kinds of dirty plans that involved me.

I swallowed the lump in my throat. It was the first time in my life that I was going through something similar.

The game called spin the bottle was one of my specialties. I always won when we were playing it.

"Well, I guess that means I'm going to have to go through the punishment that you're brewing for me."

Amelia put her finger on her chin. "It's a surprise. Since you can't back down anymore, you have no choice but to go through with it."

I swallowed another lump in my throat. It was also the first time in my life I was feeling this nervous.

I turned my eyes back to the left, checking out the huge guy whose skin color made him look very different from everyone else in the room.

It wasn't that I was singling out that part of him, but that I had a thing for black men. There was just something about them that made ripples of pleasure run through my body.

He wasn't just tall but also had a muscular body unlike any other. Muscles on top of muscles, curves in all the right places, big hands, big feet – and we all knew what that meant, a huge bulge in his groin region, a sleeveless shirt that clung to his body, showing me his perfect abs even though he was seated on the carpet, and biceps that could make any man's feel worthless in comparison.

I wasn't going to say that I was gay or anything like that. In fact, I wasn't. I was even engaged to my girlfriend. We were going to marry soon and I was making all kinds of preparations for that.

I just didn't think that I was going to be meeting someone that allured me and made me afraid of him.

"Well, I know about that. That's why I signed under the fine print." I took a deep breath in. "And are you not going to tell me what it is that I need to do? You know that next week I need to go back home."

She giggled, covering her mouth with her hand. "Don't worry. It will all happen when the time is right."

My hands were sweaty. "I don't like the sound of that at all, but I'll play along."

She rubbed her hands together. "That's what I like to hear. You are my friend. The only thing you need to keep in mind is that I'm not going to do anything that you don't like."

Well, it wasn't like I could tell her what my true feelings for her were. I wasn't going to deny that she looked nothing short of stunning.

Perfect lips, big boobs, smooth skin that shone even under the moonlight coming through the windows, and hair that fell around her face and made it stand out more than it already did.

If someone said that he had a crush on her, I wouldn't hold it against him. She was a stunning woman in pretty much everything she did or was.

After a pause, I said, "Well, just tell me what it is already. Now I'm getting curious."

She turned her eyes to look at the big man whose name I didn't know.

"I think I'm going to start with something easy for you to do. I don't want to scare you."

"Something easy for me to do? And you are not telling me that it involves him, right?"

She nodded, grinning from ear to ear again.

"Bayden, take off your pants. I want him to touch you. I want him to jack you off."

I blinked twice. I couldn't believe what she was saying. "Wait Amelia, you didn't say that it was going to involve something sexual. I thought I was just going to-"

She shook her head. "You still remember everything I said we were going to do, right? If you lost the game, you would have to do anything I wanted, and that included going through a transformation that is going to change your life completely."

I scrunched up my eyebrows. "Wait, you can't be serious about this. You can do something like that? You can change my gender?"

She nodded quickly and hastily. "I can do that and a lot more. You're going to be surprised by everything I can do with just a pill."

I swallowed another lump in my throat. I could still back away from this, but for me, it was also a matter of honor.

I wanted to find out if she was really telling the truth. I just couldn't wrap my head around it. There was no way she could make me a woman.

Bayden snuck his fingers under his pants, standing up and then taking them off. I was mesmerized, finally seeing what his legs looked like.

Each one of them was thicker than my two legs combined, and I wouldn't say that I was a skinny man. I was very typical in that regard, I thought.

Well, I needed to go on. No chickening out this time.

CHAPTER 2

ayden put his fingers under the bands of his white boxers and pulled it down. Still mesmerized by everything I was seeing, it was like I was traveling to another world. A world where I wasn't a man anymore.

It wasn't just that his legs were thick and very muscular, but also that they were just perfect.

Toned, hairy, skin the color of dark chocolate, his calves looking like something I'd see in gym commercials only, and he looked like someone that played soccer often.

Pulling down his boxers, I gasped when I saw his massive, girthy cock jumping out of them. It was bouncing up and down when he slid the band of the boxers over the head. He was cut, and there was a bead of his pre-come already coming out through the slit.

I didn't know he was already hard even though we didn't start things properly yet.

"Holy shit. It's too big."

And I wasn't exaggerating. He had to be at least nine inches in length and his balls... Damn. It looked like they were heavy and filled with his milk. I wondered what he could do with them, how long it would take him to empty them while he came all over my face. I knew I was being a slut and all, but I couldn't contain those thoughts appearing in my mind.

I took another long, careful look at his man tool. Veins all over the surface, his pre-come leaking out, his scrotum filled with curvy, rugged lines, some pubic hair but not a lot of it – he trimmed before tonight, which meant he already knew that this was going to be happening – and the skin looking taught. I could only think that it all meant he'd been preparing for this moment.

"Scoot over. I see that look in your eyes. There is no point lying to me about it. You want Bayden, don't you?" Amelia asked, turning her grin into a gentle, comforting smile. It was like she was teasing me to do what she wanted, which was to give that huge BBC the blowjob it craved.

I swallowed again. I felt and I knew that I was much smaller than he was. No comparison could be made without undervaluing his size.

Putting my hands on the floor, I crawled up to him. My body was heavier than normal, but it was okay. I was going to get through this.

Bayden sat on the floor, one of his hands wrapping around the circumference of his massive, heavy dick. He pulled down at the skin, making it look more taught while the veins popped out.

He knew what he was doing, and he wasn't ashamed of that at all. If anything, it was making him feel more confident about what he could do.

I was so close to him now that I could hear his breathing. I didn't want to focus on that because I knew that I didn't want to feel that I was gay. I wasn't, dammit! Or at least that was what I was hammering in my mind.

"Can I do this, master?" I asked. For some reason, even though I was aware of the engagement ring on my finger, it felt right to say that.

He curled up the corner of his lips. He didn't say anything, but I knew that he was giving me the green light.

Moving his hand away, he gave me all the space to do what needed to be done.

After this, there was also going to be the gender transformation part. My heart was hammering in my chest. I couldn't wait to find out if that was true or not.

I wrapped my fingers around his manhood, feeling how warm and thick it was. I couldn't make it so my thumb was touching my other fingers, and that was a first in my life.

The mere fact of grabbing his dick like this was showing me that Bayden was more like a man that needed to be worshipped. Nobody could be compared to someone of his size.

I lowered the skin and pulled it back up, feeling like I was turning gay. Well, if this wasn't doing that, then I didn't know what would. I could see another bead of his pre-come coming out of the slit.

At this moment, I felt like Amelia wasn't even with us anymore, even though I knew that couldn't be true. She had to be here somewhere. I was sure of it.

He lowered his hand, putting it on mine. "I'm going to help you with this."

Lowering his hand, he made my hand go all the way down, until my fingers were touching the skin of his scrotum. I could feel how warm that part of his body was. Moments later, he moved it back up and then down again, making sure that he was doing it slowly and carefully.

Bayden was aware that this was the first time I was doing this. He didn't want to scare me. The most curious thing about this? It was that it was making me hard even though I shouldn't be. I couldn't even see the face of my girlfriend in my head. It was like she didn't exist to me anymore.

Picking up the pace, his shaft was getting warmer and warmer as time passed. His balls were beginning to feel the rhythm of what we were doing.

Bayden was already close to coming when I put my hand around his shaft, and I knew that now he was even closer.

Moments later, he erupted, shooting rope after rope of his milk in the air. It fell onto his shirt, legs, and my hands. It was so thick and white that I knew he was the kind of man that could make several women pregnant in a row.

I didn't say that to him, of course. I would never be able to say that while keeping a straight face.

Not to mention that he was already pointing with his finger at what he wanted me to do next. I curled my fingers away and retreated my hand.

Putting my tongue out, I lowered my head and started to lick up his semen. Amelia never mentioned that I had to do this, but it still felt right. It was the first time that I was tasting another man's cum.

And the best thing about that? It was that what I was doing felt right.

CHAPTER 3

I cracked my eyes open. My heart was a little tight and my head was still a little heavy, but it was okay. Looking from left to right, I realized that I was still in the same house and room as before. It was Halloween night, and I could hear everyone playing outside. Pranks, trick-or-treating, scaring other people, and that sort of stuff.

Meanwhile, my Halloween night was going to be about me finding out if the pill did the thing that it was supposed to do. Turning me into a woman… I never thought that it was real, but I was going to find out now anyway.

That was why I was lying in bed, covered by a comforter. I moved my hand down my chest, realizing that it already felt different than it was before.

Where it was flat no more than a couple of hours ago, now it was round with something kind of sticking out in the middle.

I put two of my fingers on it, tweezing it and groaning when I felt that familiar, rough texture that could only mean one thing. It was a nipple. Bigger, thicker, and harder than my older nipples. I could already tell that Amelia hadn't been lying when she said the pill was indeed going to make me a woman.

I moved my hand, putting it on my boob. Enclosing it, I couldn't help but give it a little squeeze. Pleasure rippled through my body, making me moan like never before in my life. It was one thing grabbing and squeezing my girlfriend's boobs, and another to be doing the same to my own breasts.

I couldn't wrap my head around the perfection of everything

that I thought this meant.

Finding that what I was doing wasn't enough, I lifted my other hand and placed it on my second breast. Digging my fingers into the skin, I decided to give it another squeeze that shot more pleasure through my body. I even arched my back, already making all kinds of plans for when I jumped off the bed.

A gentle, tight-lipped smile appeared on my face. Now that I had two breasts, I was going to do unimaginable things with them.

Making circles on my boobs, I started to moan and groan like this was the last thing I was doing with my life. I was squirming under the comforter, the bed creaking under my weight. I was so into what I was doing that I wasn't even paying attention to the level of noise I was making.

And I felt a flame of heat rising in my body, spreading through it when, suddenly, it exploded. It rushed through every cell of mine, making my breathing raggedy and hard.

When I reopened my eyes and came back to what was happening around me, where I was, I realized that I was still the same person from before. Still the same guy… or gal, I thought with a smile on my face.

"Damn… It was a lot better than I thought it was going to be," I murmured, my breathing finally calming down.

And I realized that I was still alone. Alone in the house, and with the possibility of doing whatever I wanted right now.

Which meant… Lowering my hand and finding out if I also had the most important thing about being a woman. A pussy. Just the thought that I might have it now was already making me salivate.

Gliding my hand down the skin of my belly, I touched what appeared to be the pubic hair of my cunt. I couldn't find the pole sticking out that had always been there before, which made me feel more excited about the possibility of the pill indeed having changed that in my body as well.

Lowering my hand further down, I found a slit. I prodded it with my finger, pushing the right side of the slit to the right and feeling a surge of pleasure going through every part of my body when I realized that what I was feeling could only mean one thing.

"Holy shit…" I murmured. "It worked."

And I wasn't lying to myself. My fanny was there, and there was also something else that was sticking out. It was small, much smaller than my cock, but that was exactly what I thought it was going to be like.

My clitoris. My clit. My bundle of nerves.

Swiping my finger over it, I squirmed when I felt another wave of pleasure going through the entirety of my body. My cock had been replaced by my clit, and after giving it that swipe, I knew that I was finally going to regain the pleasure of masturbating myself.

Giving it another swipe, I noticed someone coming up to the door. I had no idea if it was someone that was going to open it, but in my mind, I was thinking – and hoping - that it was Bayden.

I couldn't wait until I was pleasing him differently this time. I was pretty sure that he would look at me and think that I was much more appetizing than before.

He was just that kind of man.

CHAPTER 4

The door opened and my eyes went to the right. I knew who I was going to find because of the heavy sound of his footsteps. He was standing there like a mountain, bigger than any other man I'd seen in my life.

When his eyes went to the left, a smile appeared on his face. It was a dirty, raunchy, and naughty smile. It was everything I thought it was going to be.

"I see that the transformation is already over. Ready to play with me?"

He didn't even need to ask. I was already pushing away my comforter. The room was dark, but his eyes were much better than mine.

He could see all the curves, the lines that defined my body, my boobs, and my ass. And he was loving everything that he was seeing.

"Come to me, Daddy. Do everything you want to do with me," I said, squirming and closing my legs. I was just teasing him. It wasn't like I could make this difficult for him. Once he was right on top of me, he'd push them open with all of his strength, and I knew that he wasn't going to be gentle with me.

He widened his smile. "I knew you were going to say that," he said, padding over to me without closing the door. It was like he wanted more people to come here and find out what was happening.

I was kind of growing afraid of him and what he might do. I knew that my life was going to be wholly different from now on.

"Open those legs. I want to see what you are hiding there," he ordered and I didn't obey. I knew that it wasn't going to last long, but that was okay.

He widened his smile again. "Don't make this more difficult for you than it already is," he warned, and all I could see was the big cock between his legs. It was pointing right at me, and it felt right to be doing this with him when I was finally a woman.

He climbed up on the bed, his weight making the mattress sink and bounce back up. He grabbed me with his strong, confident hands, pulled me to him, and then shoved open my legs.

"Oh my..." He said through gritted teeth. He was finally staring at what was between my legs and the shine in his eyes was telling me everything that he was thinking. He was already hard when he came into the room and now he was even harder.

"It's for you..." It was the only thing I could say right now. I knew that he was going to make me feel impossible things with that big, massive cock of his.

"I did right by waiting for this moment. I knew that I was going to be well-rewarded for my patience."

Bayden was already sweating, drops of sweat pooling over his body, tracing the curves and the lines of it, his muscles shining under the fuzzy moonlight coming through the windows. I could look into his eyes for hours on end if I didn't know that he was going to sink that shaft of his inside me now.

A bead of pre-come coming out through the slit...

His veins bulging out and pumping his blood...

His cockhead was still pointing right at me, and even though I didn't measure his size, I knew he was so thick that he was going to stretch my womb and make it feel less tight than it was.

He took a deep breath in and I knew that he was admiring what he was seeing in front of his eyes. His hands, still grabbing my legs, were doing so without hurting me. I knew that he wasn't the kind of person that would hurt me unless he had to, or unless it was something he couldn't avoid.

"This is going to hurt a little," he mumbled, pulling me closer to him until he was prodding the entrance of my pussy with his dong.

I squirmed, my back arching. He hadn't even breached me yet, and I was wondering what I would feel when he was popping my hymen.

"Don't worry about how much it's going to hurt me. I want every inch of you," I said, the only thing that I knew right now was that I wanted him ramming in and out of me.

"I wasn't worried about that," he said, pulling me even closer to him until the head of his dick was breaching through the first barrier. He was forcing it in. It was the first time in my life that I was feeling this wet. It was also the first time that I noticed that the bedsheets were so wet. This was the first time for a lot of things in my life.

He kept making his way inside of me, stopping when he noticed that his cockhead found something. My hymen, I thought.

And if I'd thought that he was going to be gentle with that part, then I'd been a fool. He threw his hips forward, breaking through that part of my body like it didn't mean anything to him. And I had to say that that was true.

Bayden kept pulling me towards him, yanking me to his hips while the veins in his arms popped out again. He stopped only when he encountered some resistance he thought wasn't there. The end of my womb.

And I looked down, realizing that he hadn't been able to slot the entirety of his impressive, girthy dong inside of me. Holy shit.

I'd thought he was nine inches long before, but now I realized that he was much bigger than that. It was like he was 10 or maybe even eleven inches in length.

And he was stretching me so hard, filling me so completely I knew it would be difficult when he wasn't inside of me anymore. I knew that this moment would end eventually, but I wasn't letting that ruin what I was feeling.

A lot of pain, but also a lot of pleasure.

And right now, I just had one thing to say to him, "Fuck my brain out."

CHAPTER 5

"I didn't think it was going to be like this," I said, feeling like stars were exploding in my mind. He was so big, so thick, so massive that he was making me wonder if, when someone else was fucking me, I would feel the same way I was feeling now.

"This isn't even the beginning," he said, rolling his hips slowly and carefully at the start. It was only the beginning and I knew that soon he was going to be picking up the pace.

And when he was doing that, I knew he would fuck me so hard it would be difficult to return to my old self.

I lowered my hands, finding my boobs and squeezing them. Bayden smiled, still pounding in and out of me slowly and carefully.

Even though he was trying not to hurt me, he was still making me feel a lot of pain. It was surging through my whole body.

Then, moving my right hand slightly to the left, I pinched one of my nipples. My other hand went to my clit and I started to give it strong, confident swipes that were making it harder than it already was.

"Hmm… you're so desperate it's kind of funny," he murmured, lowering his head and licking my bundle of nerves. Moving his hand to it, he started to rub it and make me feel things wilder than I thought possible. He wasn't just doing me now. He was turning me into his doll, and I knew that was the only thing I wanted in my life right now.

"You're more than I thought you were. You're so good fucking me like this," I said, feeling that speaking right now was more difficult than I thought it was.

"It's only the beginning of everything that I have planned for you. What do you think about getting pregnant? I can put a life inside of you."

I widened my eyes. "It's actually everything I want, other than you fucking me for hours on end. You are the only person I know that can do that."

"You're right about that," he murmured after lowering his head and putting his lips so close to my ear that I could feel his hot, minty breath on my face.

What we said seemed to have ignited a stronger and more potent fire inside of him. He started to pick up the pace, his balls slapping off my buttocks and ripples of pleasure waving through my body.

My body went into a frenetic frenzy when I came. I couldn't control what it was doing. And I was just realizing that women came a lot harder than men did. It was my experience anyway.

When it stopped, he snuck his hand to the crook of my neck. He stopped pounding in and out of me, holding me still for a moment.

"Hope you still have a lot of energy left in you. I'm not done yet," he growled into my ear, resuming what he was doing with the same impetus from before. It didn't look like he could be stopped.

I came not just once, but several times in a row. I was matching him thrust for thrust, and it was one of the best experiences of my life. I was gripping the bedsheets with all I could, but everything was still a lot tougher than I thought it was going to be.

Seconds later, he was erupting inside my cunt. I was clenching it tightly around him. Letting go of it? The thought wasn't even crossing my mind. The only thing I wanted to do right now was to keep being one with him. Our connection couldn't be severed.

Except that it looked like he had other plans in mind. He finished filling my womb with his milk and was now looking to do something else.

The big black man pulled out of me, flipping me around on the bed and lining up his dick to my face. Not having much time to react, I didn't plan on what I was going to do now with him. It was more than evident that he was going to unload the rest of his come all over my face, and I couldn't wait until he was doing so.

"Please... have mercy on me," I pleaded, placing a finger on my bottom lip. I was pretending that what he was doing was hurting me.

It wasn't. The more I fantasized about this BBC, the more I realized he was the right one.

He enclosed his dick with his hands, pumping it with a big smile on his face.

"You want this, don't you? You want every single drop," he said without hiding the smile that appeared on his face. It was the smile of a man that didn't care about anyone but himself.

"Yes, please..." I begged and in a moment his dick was sputtering out his thick, dense, and warm milk all over me. It wasn't hitting just my face, but also all over me.

It was so hot that it was almost burning my skin and even though I didn't think that was a normal reaction to be having right now, I didn't give it much thought.

"Damn..." Bayden muttered to himself, giving his dong one more strong stroke before crawling off the bed. I thought that he was going to plop down on it as I did, but it looked like he had other plans in mind.

He was leaving me alone, and I didn't think that things were going to end there. If anything, I knew he'd be back soon, breaching his sissy again.

The End

Leave a review if you liked the book. It really helps me!

MORE SISSY STORIES

SERIES – FEMININE FOR A MISTRESS

1. Sissy Has Logged In: Online for Domination and Submission
2. My Little Doll: From Man to Sissy
3. From King to Sissy: A Steamy Sissification Story
4. Once a Sissy, Always a Sissy: A Filthy Feminization Story
5. Sissy Curves: A Taboo Feminization Story
6. Sissy Backdoor: A Rough Submission Feminization Story
7. Sissy Wishes: A Taboo Feminization Femdom Story

SERIES – CHANGED

1. This is so Wrong: A First Time Sissification Story
2. I'm Going to Hell for This: A First Time Sissification Story
3. I'm Going to Regret This: A First Time Feminization Story
4. No Coming Back: A Sissification Story
5. Christmas Sissy: A Feminization BDSM Story

FEMINIZATION BUNDLES

Tight Sissies Bundle: 6 Filthy Feminization Stories
Merciless Rear Entrance Sharing: 9 Dirty Stories of Bimbofication, Cuckold, Sissification, Menage, Harem and MORE

FUTA ON FEMALE STORIES

ABOUT THE AUTHOR

Leandra's Camilli's obsession? Writing dirty, steamy stories that will make you drool. She loves her Alpha males, hucows, sissies, and futas. If you're looking for that kind of book, you've found the right author page.

With a cup of coffee on her table and warm socks on, she writes almost every day. Leandra Camilli's been present in several top 100 categories in the store, and she always finishes her stories.